The Angels of Mons

The Angels of Mons

THE BOWMEN

AND OTHER

LEGENDS OF THE WAR

BY

ARTHUR MACHEN

WITH AN INTRODUCTION BY THE AUTHOR

Short Story Index Reprint Series

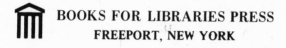

BOOKS FOR LIBRARIES PRESS
FREEPORT, NEW YORK

First Published 1915
Reprinted 1972

Library of Congress Cataloging in Publication Data

Machen, Arthur, 1863-1947.
    The angels of Mons.

    (Short story index reprint series)
    CONTENTS: The bowmen.--The soldiers' rest.--The
monstrance. [etc.]
    1. European War, 1914-1918--Fiction. I. Title.
II. Title: The bowmen.
PZ3.M183An6 [PR6025.A245]   823'.9'12   72-4474
ISBN 0-8369-4183-7

PRINTED IN THE UNITED STATES OF AMERICA

CONTENTS

v

THE BOWMEN

INTRODUCTION

I HAVE been asked to write an introduction to the story of "The Bowmen," on its publication in book form together with three other tales of similar fashion. And I hesitate. This affair of "The Bowmen" has been such an odd one from first to last, so many queer complications have entered into it, there have been so many and so divers currents and cross-currents of rumour and speculation concerning it, that I honestly do not know where to begin. I propose, then, to solve the difficulty by apologizing for beginning at all.

For, usually and fitly, the presence of

an introduction is held to imply that there is something of consequence and importance to be introduced. If, for example, a man has made an anthology of great poetry, he may well write an introduction justifying his principle of selection, pointing out here and there, as the spirit moves him, high beauties and supreme excellencies, discoursing of the magnates and lords and princes of literature, whom he is merely serving as groom of the chamber. Introductions, that is, belong to the masterpieces and classics of the world, to the great and ancient and accepted things; and I am here introducing a short, small story of my own which appeared in THE EVENING NEWS *about ten months ago.*

I appreciate the absurdity, nay, the enormity of the position in all its grossness. And my excuse for these pages must be this: that though the story itself is nothing, it has yet had such odd and unforeseen conse-

quences and adventures that the tale of them may possess some interest. And then, again, there are certain psychological morals to be drawn from the whole matter of the tale and its sequel of rumours and discussions that are not, I think, devoid of consequence; and so to begin at the beginning.

This was in last August; to be more precise, on the last Sunday of last August. There were terrible things to be read on that hot Sunday morning between meat and mass. It was in THE WEEKLY DISPATCH that I saw the awful account of the retreat from Mons. I no longer recollect the details; but I have not forgotten the impression that was then made on my mind. I seemed to see a furnace of torment and death and agony and terror seven times heated, and in the midst of the burning was the British Army. In the midst of the flame, consumed by it and yet aureoled in it, scattered like *ashes and yet triumphant, martyred and for ever glorious. So I saw our men with a shining about them, so I took these thoughts with me to church, and, I am sorry to say, was making up a story in my head while the deacon was singing the Gospel.*

This was not the tale of " The Bowmen." It was the first sketch, as it were, of " The Soldiers' Rest," which is reprinted in this volume. I only wish I had been able to write it as I conceived it. The tale as it stands is, I think, a far better piece of craft than " The Bowmen," but the tale that came to me as the blue incense floated above the Gospel Book on the desk between the tapers: that indeed was a noble story—like all the stories that never get written. I conceived the dead men coming up through the flames and in the flames, and being welcomed in the Eternal Tavern with songs and flowing cups and everlasting mirth. But every man is the child of his age, however much he may hate it; and our popular religion has long determined that jollity is wicked. As far as I can make out modern Protestantism believes that Heaven is something like Evensong in an English cathedral, the service by Stainer and the Dean preaching. For those opposed to dogma of any kind—even the mildest—I suppose it is held that a Course of Ethical Lectures will be arranged.

Well, I have long maintained that on the whole the average church, considered as a house of preaching, is a much more poisonous place than the average tavern; still, as I say, one's age masters one, and clouds and bewilders the intelligence, and the real story of "The Soldiers' Rest," with its "sonus epulantium in æterno convivio," was ruined at the moment of its birth, and it was some time later that the actual story, as here printed, got written. And in the meantime the plot of "The Bowmen" occurred to me. Now it has been murmured and hinted and suggested and whispered in all sorts of quarters that before I wrote the tale I had heard something. The most decorative of these legends is also the most precise: "I know for a fact that the whole thing was given him in typescript by a lady-in-waiting." This was not the case; and all vaguer reports to the effect that I had heard some rumours or hints of rumours are equally void of any trace of truth.

Again I apologize for entering so pompously into the minutiæ of my bit of a story, as if it were the lost poems of Sappho; but it appears that the subject interests the public, and I comply with my instructions. I take it, then, that the origins of "The Bowmen" were composite. First of all, all ages and nations have cherished the thought that spiritual hosts may come to the help of earthly arms, that gods and heroes and saints have descended from their high immortal places to fight for their worshippers and clients. Then Kipling's story of the ghostly Indian regiment got into my head and got mixed with the mediævalism that is always there; and so "The Bowmen" was written. I was heartily disappointed with it, I remember, and thought it—as I still think it —an indifferent piece of work. However, I have tried to write for these thirty-five long years, and if I have not become practised in letters, I am at least a past master in the Lodge of Disappointment. Such as it was, "The Bowmen" appeared in THE EVENING NEWS *of September 29th,* 1914.

Now the journalist does not, as a rule, dwell much on the prospect of fame; and if he be an evening journalist, his anticipations of immortality are bounded by twelve o'clock at night at the latest; and it may well be that those insects which begin to live in the morning and are dead by sunset deem themselves immortal. Having written my story, having groaned and growled over it and printed it, I certainly never thought to hear another word of it. My colleague "The Londoner" praised it warmly to my face, as his kindly fashion is; entering, very properly, a technical caveat as to the language of the battle-cries of the bowmen. "Why should English archers use French terms?" he said. I replied that the only reason was this—that a "Monseigneur" here and there struck me as picturesque; and I reminded him that, as a matter of cold historical fact, most of the archers of Agincourt were mercenaries from Gwent, my native country, who would appeal to Mihangel and to saints not known to the Saxons—Teilo, Iltyd, Dewi, Cadwaladyr Vendigeid. And I thought that that was the first and last discussion of "The Bowmen." But in a few days from its publication the editor of THE OCCULT REVIEW *wrote to me. He wanted to know whether the story had any foundation in fact. I told him that it had no foundation in fact of any kind or sort; I forget whether I added that it had no foundation in rumour, but I should think not, since to the best of my belief there were no rumours of heavenly interposition in existence at that time. Certainly I had heard of none. Soon afterwards the editor of LIGHT wrote asking a like question, and I made him a like reply. It seemed to me that I had stifled any "Bowmen" mythos in the hour of its birth.*

A month or two later, I received several requests from editors of parish magazines to reprint the story. I—or, rather, my editor—readily gave permission; and then, after another month or two, the conductor of one of these magazines wrote to me, saying that the February issue containing the story had been sold out, while there was still a great demand for it. Would I allow them to reprint "The Bowmen" as a pamphlet, and would I write a short preface giving the exact authorities for the story? I replied that they might reprint in pamphlet form with all my heart, but that I could not give my authorities, since I had none, the tale being pure invention. The priest wrote again, suggesting—to my amazement —that I must be mistaken, that the main "facts" of "The Bowmen" must be true, that my share in the matter must surely have been confined to the elaboration and decoration of a veridical history. It seemed that my light fiction had been accepted by the congregation of this particular church as the solidest of facts; and it was then that it began to dawn on me that if I had failed in the art of letters, I had succeeded, unwittingly, in the art of deceit. This happened, I should think, some time in April, and the snowball of rumour that was then set rolling has been rolling ever since, growing bigger and bigger, till it is now swollen to a monstrous size.

It was at about this period that variants of my tale began to be told as authentic histories. At first, these tales betrayed their relation to their original. In several of them the vegetarian restaurant appeared, and St. George was the chief character. In one case an officer—name and address miss-ing—said that there was a portrait of St. George in a certain London restaurant, and that a figure, just like the portrait, appeared to him on the battlefield, and was invoked by him, with the happiest results. Another variant—this, I think, never got into print— told how dead Prussians had been found on the battlefield with arrow wounds in their bodies. This notion amused me, as I had imagined a scene, when I was thinking out the story, in which a German general was to appear before the Kaiser to explain his failure to annihilate the English.

"All-Highest," the general was to say, "it is true, it is impossible to deny it. The

men were killed by arrows; the shafts were found in their bodies by the burying parties."

I rejected the idea as over-precipitous even for a mere fantasy. I was therefore entertained when I found that what I had refused as too fantastical for fantasy was accepted in certain occult circles as hard fact.

Other versions of the story appeared in which a cloud interposed between the attacking Germans and the defending British. In some examples the cloud served to conceal our men from the advancing enemy; in others, it disclosed shining shapes which frightened the horses of the pursuing German cavalry. St. George, it will be noted, has disappeared—he persisted some time longer in certain Roman Catholic variants— and there are no more bowmen, no more arrows. But so far angels are not mentioned; yet they are ready to appear, and I think that I have detected the machine which brought them into the story.

In "The Bowmen" my imagined soldier saw "a long line of shapes, with a shining about them." And Mr. A. P. Sinnett, writing in the May issue of THE OCCULT REVIEW, *reporting what he had heard, states that "those who could see said they saw 'a row of shining beings' between the two armies." Now I conjecture that the word "shining" is the link between my tale and the derivative from it. In the popular view shining and benevolent supernatural beings are angels and nothing else, and must be angels, and so, I believe, the Bowmen of my story have become "the Angels of Mons." In this shape they have been received with respect and credence everywhere, or almost everywhere.*

And here, I conjecture, we have the key to the large popularity of the delusion—as I think it. We have long ceased in England to take much interest in saints, and in the recent revival of the cultus of St. George, the saint is little more than a patriotic figure-head. And the appeal to the saints to succour us is certainly not a common English practice; it is held Popish by most of our countrymen. But angels, with certain reservations, have retained their popularity, and so, when it was settled that the English army in its dire peril was delivered by angelic aid, the way was clear for general belief, and for the enthusiasms of the religion of the man in the street. And so soon as the legend got the title "The Angels of Mons" it became impossible to avoid it. It permeated the Press: it would not be neglected; it appeared in the most unlikely quarters—in Truth *and* Town Topics, The New Church Weekly (*Sweden-borgian*) *and* John Bull. *The editor of* The Church Times *has exercised a wise reserve: he awaits that evidence which* so

*far is lacking; but in one issue of the paper
I noted that the story furnished a text for a
sermon, the subject of a letter, and the matter
for an article. People send me cuttings
from provincial papers containing hot con-
troversy as to the exact nature of the ap-
pearances; the "Office Window" of* The
Daily Chronicle *suggests scientific explanations of the hallucination; the* Pall
Mall *in a note about St. James says he is
of the brotherhood of the Bowmen of Mons—
this reversion to the bowmen from the angels
being possibly due to the strong statements
that I have made on the matter. The
pulpits both of the Church and of Noncon-
formity have been busy: Bishop Welldon,
Dean Hensley Henson (a disbeliever),
Bishop Taylor Smith (the Chaplain-Gen-
eral), and many other clergy have occupied
themselves with the matter. Dr. Horton
preached about the "angels" at Manchester;
Sir Joseph Compton Rickett (President of*

the National Federation of Free Church Councils) stated that the soldiers at the front had seen visions and dreamed dreams, and had given testimony of powers and principalities fighting for them or against them. Letters come from all the ends of the earth to the editor of THE EVENING NEWS *with theories, beliefs, explanations, suggestions. It is all somewhat wonderful; one can say that the whole affair is a psychological phenomenon of considerable interest, fairly comparable with the great Russian delusion of last August and September.*

.   .   .   .   .

Now it is possible that some persons, judging by the tone of these remarks of mine, may gather the impression that I am a profound disbeliever in the possibility of any intervention of the superphysical order in the affairs of the physical order. They will be mistaken if they make this inference;

they will be mistaken if they suppose that I think miracles in Judæa credible but miracles in France or Flanders incredible. I hold no such absurdities. But I confess, very frankly, that I credit none of the "Angels of Mons" legends, partly because I see, or think I see, their derivation from my own idle fiction, but chiefly because I have, so far, not received one jot or tittle of evidence that should dispose me to belief. It is idle, indeed, and foolish enough for a man to say: "I am sure that story is a lie, because the supernatural element enters into it"; here, indeed, we have the maggot writhing in the midst of corrupted offal denying the existence of the sun. But if this fellow be a fool—as he is—equally foolish is he who says: "If the tale has anything of the supernatural it is true, and the less evidence the better"; and I am afraid this tends to be the attitude of many who call themselves occultists. I hope that I shall never get to

2

that frame of mind. So I say, not that supernormal interventions are impossible, not that they have not happened during this war—I know nothing as to that point, one way or the other—but that there is not one atom of evidence (so far) to support the current stories of the angels of Mons. For, be it remarked, these stories are specific stories. They rest on the second, third, fourth, fifth hand stories told by "a soldier," by "an officer," by "a Catholic correspondent," by "a nurse," by any number of anonymous people. Indeed, names have been mentioned. A lady's name has been drawn, most unwarrantably as it appears to me, into the discussion, and I have no doubt that this lady has been subject to a good deal of pestering and annoyance. She has written to the editor of THE EVENING NEWS *denying all knowledge of the supposed miracle. The Psychical Research Society's expert confesses that no real evi-*

dence has been proffered to her Society on the matter. And then, to my amazement, she accepts as fact the proposition that some men on the battlefield have been "hallucinated," and proceeds to give the theory of sensory hallucination. She forgets that, by her own showing, there is no reason to suppose that anybody has been hallucinated at all. Someone (unknown) has met a nurse (unnamed) who has talked to a soldier (anonymous) who has seen angels. But THAT *is not evidence; and not even Sam Weller at his gayest would have dared to offer it as such in the Court of Common Pleas. So far, then, nothing remotely approaching proof has been offered as to any supernatural intervention during the Retreat from Mons. Proof may come; if so, it will be interesting and more than interesting.*

But, taking the affair as it stands at present, how is it that a nation plunged in materialism of the grossest kind has accepted idle rumours and gossip of the supernatural as certain truth? The answer is contained in the question: it is precisely because our whole atmosphere is materialist that we are ready to credit anything—save the truth. Separate a man from good drink, he will swallow methylated spirit with joy. Man is created to be inebriated; to be "nobly wild, not mad." Suffer the Cocoa Prophets and their company to seduce him in body and spirit, and he will get himself stuff that will make him ignobly wild and mad indeed. It took hard, practical men of affairs, business men, advanced thinkers, Freethinkers, to believe in Madame Blavatsky and Mahatmas and the famous message from the Golden Shore: "Judge's plan is right; follow him and STICK."

And the main responsibility for this dismal state of affairs undoubtedly lies on the shoulders of the majority of the clergy of the Church of England. Christianity, as Mr. W. L. Courtney has so admirably pointed out, is a great Mystery Religion; it is THE *Mystery Religion. Its priests are called to an awful and tremendous hierurgy; its pontiffs are to be the path-finders, the bridge-makers between the world of sense and the world of spirit. And, in fact, they pass their time in preaching, not the eternal mysteries, but a twopenny morality, in changing the Wine of Angels and the Bread of Heaven into gingerbeer and mixed biscuits: a sorry transubstantiation, a sad alchemy, as it seems to me.*

THE BOWMEN

IT was during the Retreat of the Eighty Thousand, and the authority of the Censorship is sufficient excuse for not being more explicit. But it was on the most awful day of that awful time, on the day when ruin and disaster came so near that their shadow fell over London far away; and, without any certain news, the hearts of men failed within them and grew faint; as if the agony of the army in the battlefield had entered into their souls.

On this dreadful day, then, when three hundred thousand men in arms with all their artillery swelled like a flood against the little English company, there was one point above all other points in our battle line that was for a time in awful danger, not merely of defeat, but of utter annihilation. With the permission of the Censorship and of the military expert, this corner may, perhaps, be described as a salient, and if this angle were crushed and broken, then the English force as a whole would be shattered, the Allied left would be turned, and Sedan would inevitably follow.

All the morning the German guns had thundered and shrieked against this corner, and against the thousand or so of men who held it. The men joked at the shells, and found funny names for them, and had bets about them, and greeted them with scraps of music-hall songs. But the shells came on and burst, and tore good English-men limb from limb, and tore brother from brother, and as the heat of the day increased so did the fury of that terrific cannonade. There was no help, it seemed. The English artillery was good, but there was not nearly enough of it; it was being steadily battered into scrap iron.

There comes a moment in a storm at sea when people say to one another, "It is at its worst; it can blow no harder," and then there is a blast ten times more fierce than any before it. So it was in these British trenches.

There were no stouter hearts in the whole world than the hearts of these men; but even they were appalled as this seven-times-heated hell of the German cannonade fell upon them and overwhelmed them and destroyed them. And at this very moment they saw from their trenches that a tremendous host was moving against their lines. Five hundred of the thousand remained, and as far as they could see the German infantry was pressing on against them, column upon column, a grey world of men, ten thousand of them, as it appeared afterwards.

There was no hope at all. They shook hands, some of them. One man improvised a new version of the battle-song, "Good-bye, good-bye to Tipperary," ending with "And we shan't get there." And they all went on firing steadily. The officers pointed out that such an opportunity for high-class fancy shooting might never occur again; the Germans dropped line after line; the Tipperary humourist asked, "What price Sidney Street?" And the few machine guns did their best. But everybody knew it was of no use. The dead grey bodies lay in companies and battalions, as others came on and on and on, and they swarmed and stirred and advanced from beyond and beyond.

"World without end. Amen," said one of the British soldiers with some irrelevance as he took aim and fired. And then he remembered—he says he cannot think why or wherefore—a queer vegetarian restaurant in London where he had once or twice eaten eccentric dishes of cutlets made of lentils and nuts that pretended to be steak. On all the plates in this restaurant there was printed a figure of St. George in blue, with the motto, *Adsit Anglis Sanctus Georgius*— May St. George be a present help to the English. This soldier happened to know Latin and other useless things, and now, as he fired at his man in the grey advancing mass—three hundred yards away— he uttered the pious vegetarian motto. He went on firing to the end, and at last Bill on his right had to clout him cheerfully over the head to make him stop, pointing out as he did so that the King's ammunition cost money and was not lightly to be wasted in drilling funny patterns into dead Germans.

For as the Latin scholar uttered his invocation he felt something between

a shudder and an electric shock pass
through his body.   The roar of the battle
died down in his ears to a gentle murmur;
instead of it, he says, he heard a great
voice and a shout louder than a thunder-
peal crying, "Array, array, array!"

His heart grew hot as a burning coal,
it grew cold as ice within him, as it seemed
to him that a tumult of voices answered
to his summons.   He heard, or seemed to
hear, thousands shouting: "St. George!
St. George!"

"Ha! messire; ha! sweet Saint, grant
us good deliverance!"

"St. George for merry England!"

"Harow! Harow!   Monseigneur St.
George, succour us."

"Ha! St. George! Ha! St. George!
a long bow and a strong bow."

"Heaven's Knight, aid us!"

And as the soldier heard these voices
he saw before him, beyond the trench, a

long line of shapes, with a shining about them. They were like men who drew the bow, and with another shout, their cloud of arrows flew singing and tingling through the air towards the German hosts.

.   .   .   .   .

The other men in the trench were firing all the while. They had no hope; but they aimed just as if they had been shooting at Bisley.

Suddenly one of them lifted up his voice in the plainest English.

"Gawd help us!" he bellowed to the man next to him, "but we're blooming marvels! Look at those grey . . . gentlemen, look at them! D'ye see them? They're not going down in dozens nor in 'undreds; it's thousands, it is. Look! look! there's a regiment gone while I'm talking to ye."

"Shut it!" the other soldier bellowed, taking aim, "what are ye gassing about?"

But he gulped with astonishment even as he spoke, for, indeed, the grey men were falling by the thousands. The English could hear the guttural scream of the German officers, the crackle of their revolvers as they shot the reluctant; and still line after line crashed to the earth.

.   .   .   .   .

All the while the Latin-bred soldier heard the cry:

"Harow! Harow! Monseigneur, dear saint, quick to our aid! St. George help us!"

"High Chevalier, defend us!"

The singing arrows fled so swift and thick that they darkened the air; the heathen horde melted from before them.

.   .   .   .   .

"More machine guns!" Bill yelled to Tom.

"Don't hear them," Tom yelled back. "But, thank God, anyway; they've got it in the neck."

In fact, there were ten thousand dead German soldiers left before that salient of the English army, and consequently there was no Sedan. In Germany, a country ruled by scientific principles, the Great General Staff decided that the contemptible English must have employed shells containing an unknown gas of a poisonous nature, as no wounds were discernible on the bodies of the dead German soldiers. But the man who knew what nuts tasted like when they called themselves steak knew also that St. George had brought his Agincourt Bowmen to help the English.

THE SOLDIERS' REST

THE soldier with the ugly wound in the head opened his eyes at last, and looked about him with an air of pleasant satisfaction.

He still felt drowsy and dazed with some fierce experience through which he had passed, but so far he could not recollect much about it. But an agreeable glow began to steal about his heart—such a glow as comes to people who have been in a tight place and have come through it better than they had expected. In its mildest form this set of emotions may be observed in passengers who have crossed the Channel on a windy day without being sick. They triumph a little internally, and are suffused with vague, kindly feelings.

The wounded soldier was somewhat of this disposition as he opened his eyes, pulled himself together, and looked about him. He felt a sense of delicious ease and repose in bones that had been racked and weary, and deep in the heart that had so lately been tormented there was an assurance of comfort—of the battle won. The thundering, roaring waves were passed; he had entered into the haven of calm waters. After fatigues and terrors that as yet he could not recollect he seemed now to be resting in the easiest of all easy chairs in a dim, low room.

In the hearth there was a glint of fire and a blue, sweet-scented puff of wood smoke; a great black oak beam roughly hewn crossed the ceiling. Through the leaded panes of the windows he saw a rich glow of sunlight, green lawns, and against the deepest and most radiant of all blue skies the wonderful far-lifted towers of a vast Gothic cathedral—mystic, rich with imagery.

"Good Lord!" he murmured to himself. "I didn't know they had such places in France. It's just like Wells. And it might be the other day when I was going past the Swan, just as it might be past that window, and asked the ostler what time it was, and he says, 'What time? Why, summer-time'; and there outside it looks like summer that would last for ever. If this was an inn they ought to call it 'The Soldiers' Rest.'"

He dozed off again, and when he opened his eyes once more a kindly looking man in some sort of black robe was standing by him.

"It's all right now, isn't it?" he said, speaking in good English.

"Yes, thank you, sir, as right as can be. I hope to be back again soon."

"Well, well; but how did you come

here? Where did you get that?" He
pointed to the wound on the soldier's
forehead.

The soldier put his hand up to his brow
and looked dazed and puzzled.

"Well, sir," he said at last, "it was
like this, to begin at the beginning. You
know how we came over in August, and
there we were in the thick of it, as you
might say, in a day or two. An awful
time it was, and I don't know how I got
through it alive. My best friend was
killed dead beside me as we lay in the
trenches. By Cambrai, I think it was.

"Then things got a little quieter for a
bit, and I was quartered in a village for
the best part of a week. She was a very
nice lady where I was, and she treated
me proper with the best of everything.
Her husband he was fighting; but she
had the nicest little boy I ever knew, a
little fellow of five, or six it might be,

and we got on splendid.   The amount of
their lingo that kid taught me—'We, we'
and 'Bong swor' and 'Commong voo
porty voo,' and all—and I taught him
English. You should have heard that
nipper say ''Arf a mo', old un'! It was
a treat.

"Then one day we got surprised.
There was about a dozen of us in the village, and two or three hundred Germans
came down on us early one morning.
They got us; no help for it.   Before we
could shoot.

.   .   .   .   .

"Well, there we were.   They tied our
hands behind our backs, and smacked our
faces and kicked us a bit, and we were
lined up opposite the house where I'd
been staying.

"And then that poor little chap broke
away from his mother, and he run out

and saw one of the Boshes, as we call them, fetch me one over the jaw with his clenched fist. Oh dear! oh dear! he might have done it a dozen times if only that little child hadn't seen him.

"He had a poor bit of a toy I'd bought him at the village shop; a toy gun it was. And out he came running, as I say, crying out something in French like 'Bad man! bad man! don't hurt my Anglish or I shoot you'; and he pointed that gun at the German soldier. The German, he took his bayonet, and he drove it right through the poor little chap's throat."

The soldier's face worked and twitched and twisted itself into a sort of grin, and he sat grinding his teeth and staring at the man in the black robe. He was silent for a little. And then he found his voice, and the oaths rolled terrible, thundering from him, as he cursed that murderous wretch, and bade him go down and burn for ever in hell. And the tears were raining down his face, and they choked him at last.

"I beg your pardon, sir, I'm sure," he said, "especially you being a minister of some kind, I suppose; but I can't help it. He was such a dear little man."

The man in black murmured something to himself: "*Pretiosa in conspectu Domini mors innocentium ejus*"—Dear in the sight of the Lord is the death of His innocents. Then he put a kind hand very gently on the soldier's shoulder.

"Never mind," said he; "I've seen some service in my time, myself. But what about that wound?"

"Oh, that; that's nothing. But I'll tell you how I got it. It was just like this. The Germans had us fair, as I tell you, and they shut us up in a barn in the village; just flung us on the ground and left us to starve seemingly. They barred up the big door of the barn, and put a sentry there, and thought we were all right.

"There were sort of slits like very narrow windows in one of the walls, and on the second day it was, I was looking out of these slits down the street, and I could see those German devils were up to mischief. They were planting their machine guns everywhere handy where an ordinary man coming up the street would never see them, but I see them, and I see the infantry lining up behind the garden walls. Then I had a sort of a notion of what was coming; and presently, sure enough, I could hear some of our chaps singing 'Hullo, hullo, hullo!' in the distance; and I says to myself, 'Not this time.'

"So I looked about me, and I found a hole under the wall; a kind of a drain I should think it was, and I found I could just squeeze through. And I got out and crept round, and away I goes running down the street, yelling for all I was worth, just as our chaps were getting round the corner at the bottom. 'Bang, bang!' went the guns, behind me and in front of me, and on each side of me, and then— bash! something hit me on the head and over I went; and I don't remember anything more till I woke up here just now."

The soldier lay back in his chair and closed his eyes for a moment. When he opened them he saw that there were other people in the room besides the minister in the black robes. One was a man in a big black cloak. He had a grim old face and a great beaky nose. He shook the soldier by the hand.

"By God! sir," he said, "you're a credit to the British Army; you're a damned fine soldier and a good man, and, by God! I'm proud to shake hands with you."

And then someone came out of the

shadow, someone in queer clothes such as the soldier had seen worn by the heralds when he had been on duty at the opening of Parliament by the King.

"Now, by Corpus Domini," this man said, "of all knights ye be noblest and gentlest, and ye be of fairest report, and now ye be a brother of the noblest brotherhood that ever was since this world's beginning, since ye have yielded dear life for your friends' sake."

The soldier did not understand what the man was saying to him. There were others, too, in strange dresses, who came and spoke to him. Some spoke in what sounded like French. He could not make it out; but he knew that they all spoke kindly and praised him.

"What does it all mean?" he said to the minister. "What are they talking about? They don't think I'd let down my pals?"

"Drink this," said the minister, and he handed the soldier a great silver cup, brimming with wine.

The soldier took a deep draught, and in that moment all his sorrows passed from him.

"What is it?" he asked?

"Vin nouveau du Royaume," said the minister. "New Wine of the Kingdom, you call it." And then he bent down and murmured in the soldier's ear.

"What," said the wounded man, "the place they used to tell us about in Sunday School? With such drink and such joy——"

His voice was hushed. For as he looked at the minister the fashion of his vesture was changed. The black robe seemed to melt away from him. He was all in armour, if armour be made of starlight, of the rose of dawn, and of

sunset fires; and he lifted up a great
sword of flame.

> Full in the midst, his Cross of Red
> Triumphant Michael brandishèd,
>   And trampled the Apostate's pride.

THE MONSTRANCE

Then it fell out in the sacring of the Mass that right as the priest heaved up the Host there came a beam redder than any rose and smote upon it, and then it was changed bodily into the shape and fashion of a Child having his arms stretched forth, as he had been nailed upon the Tree.—OLD ROMANCE.

So far things were going very well indeed. The night was thick and black and cloudy, and the German force had come three-quarters of their way or more without an alarm. There was no challenge from the English lines; and indeed the English were being kept busy by a high shell-fire on their front. This had been the German plan; and it was

44

coming off admirably. Nobody thought
that there was any danger on the left;
and so the Prussians, writhing on their
stomachs over the ploughed field, were
drawing nearer and nearer to the wood.
Once there they could establish themselves comfortably and securely during
what remained of the night; and at dawn
the English left would be hopelessly
enfiladed—and there would be another of
those movements which people who really
understand military matters call "read-
justments of our line."

The noise made by the men creeping
and crawling over the fields was drowned
by the cannonade, from the English side
as well as the German. On the English
centre and right things were indeed very
brisk; the big guns were thundering and
shrieking and roaring, the machine guns
were keeping up the very devil's racket;
the flares and illuminating shells were as

good as the Crystal Palace in the old days, as the soldiers said to one another. All this had been thought of and thought out on the other side. The German force was beautifully organized. The men who crept nearer and nearer to the wood carried quite a number of machine guns in bits on their backs; others of them had small bags full of sand; yet others big bags that were empty. When the wood was reached the sand from the small bags was to be emptied into the big bags; the machine-gun parts were to be put together, the guns mounted behind the sandbag redoubt, and then, as Major Von und Zu pleasantly observed, "the English pigs shall to gehenna-fire quickly come."

The major was so well pleased with the way things had gone that he permitted himself a very low and guttural chuckle; in another ten minutes success would be

assured. He half turned his head round
to whisper a caution about some detail
of the sandbag business to the big ser-
geant-major, Karl Heinz, who was crawling just behind him. At that instant
Karl Heinz leapt into the air with a
scream that rent through the night and
through all the roaring of the artillery.
He cried in a terrible voice, "The Glory
of the Lord!" and plunged and pitched
forward, stone dead. They said that his
face as he stood up there and cried aloud
was as if it had been seen through a sheet
of flame.

"They" were one or two out of the few
who got back to the German lines. Most
of the Prussians stayed in the ploughed
field. Karl Heinz's scream had frozen
the blood of the English soldiers, but it
had also ruined the major's plans. He
and his men, caught all unready, clumsy
with the burdens that they carried, were

shot to pieces; hardly a score of them returned. The rest of the force were at-
tended to by an English burying party.
According to custom the dead men were
searched before they were buried, and
some singular relics of the campaign were
found upon them, but nothing so singular
as Karl Heinz's diary.

He had been keeping it for some time.
It began with entries about bread and
sausage and the ordinary incidents of the
trenches; here and there Karl wrote about
an old grandfather, and a big china pipe,
and pine woods and roast goose. Then
the diarist seemed to get fidgety about his
health. Thus:

April 17.—Annoyed for some days
by murmuring sounds in my head.
I trust I shall not become deaf, like
my departed uncle Christopher.

April 20.—The noise in my head

grows worse; it is a humming sound. It distracts me; twice I have failed to hear the captain and have been reprimanded.

April 22.—So bad is my head that I go to see the doctor. He speaks of *tinnitus*, and gives me an inhaling apparatus that shall reach, he says, the middle ear.

April 25.—The apparatus is of no use. The sound is now become like the booming of a great church bell. It reminds me of the bell at St. Lambart on that terrible day of last August.

April 26.—I could swear that it is the bell of St. Lambart that I hear all the time. They rang it as the procession came out of the church.

The man's writing, at first firm enough, begins to straggle unevenly over the page at this point.   The entries show that he became convinced that he heard the bell of St. Lambart's Church ringing, though (as he knew better than most men) there had been no bell and no church at St. Lambart's since the summer of 1914. There was no village either—the whole place was a rubbish-heap.

Then the unfortunate Karl Heinz was beset with other troubles.

May 2.—I fear I am becoming ill. Today Joseph Kleist, who is next to me in the trench, asked me why I jerked my head to the right so constantly. I told him to hold his tongue; but this shows that I am noticed. I keep fancying that there is something white just beyond the range of my sight on the right hand.

May 3.—This whiteness is now quite clear, and in front of me.   All this day it has slowly passed before me. I asked Joseph Kleist if he saw a piece of newspaper just beyond the trench. He stared at me solemnly— he is a stupid fool—and said, "There is no paper."

May 4.—It looks like a white robe. There was a strong smell of incense today in the trench. No one seemed to notice it. There is decidedly a white robe, and I think I can see feet, passing very slowly before me at this moment while I write.

There is no space here for continuous extracts from Karl Heinz's diary. But to condense with severity, it would seem that he slowly gathered about himself a complete set of sensory hallucinations. First the auditory hallucination of the sound of a bell, which the doctor called *tinnitus.* Then a patch of white growing into a white robe, then the smell of incense. At last he lived in two worlds. He saw his trench, and the level before it, and the English lines; he talked with his comrades and obeyed orders, though with a certain difficulty; but he also heard the deep boom of St. Lambart's bell, and saw continually advancing towards him a white procession of little children, led by a boy who was swinging a censer. There is one extraordinary entry: "But in August those children carried no lilies; now they have lilies in their hands. Why should they have lilies?"

It is interesting to note the transition over the border line. After May 2d there is no reference in the diary to bodily illness, with two notable exceptions. Up to and including that date the sergeant knows that he is suffering from illusions; after that he accepts his hallucinations as actualities. The man who cannot see what he sees and hear what he hears is a fool. So he writes: "I ask who is singing *Ave Maria Stella*. That blockhead Friedrich Schumacher raises his crest and answers insolently that no one sings, since singing is strictly forbidden for the present."

A few days before the disastrous night expedition the last figure in the procession appeared to those sick eyes.

The old priest now comes in his golden robe, the two boys holding each side of it. He is looking just as he did when he died, save that when he walked in St. Lambart there was no shining round his head. But this is illusion and contrary to reason, since no one has a shining about his head. I must take some medicine.

Note here that Karl Heinz absolutely accepts the appearance of the martyred priest of St. Lambart as actual, while he thinks that the halo must be an illusion; and so he reverts again to his physical condition.

The priest held up both his hands, the diary states, "as if there were something between them. But there is a sort of cloud or dimness over this object, whatever it may be. My poor Aunt Kathie suffered much from her eyes in her old age."

.   .   .   .   .

One can guess what the priest of St. Lambart carried in his hands when he and the little children went out into the hot sunlight to implore mercy, while the great resounding bell of St. Lambart boomed over the plain. Karl Heinz knew what happened then; they said that it was he who killed the old priest and helped to crucify the little child against the church door. The baby was only three years old. He died calling piteously for "mummy" and "daddy."

.   .   .   .   .

And those who will may guess what Karl Heinz saw when the mist cleared from before the monstrance in the priest's hands. Then he shrieked and died.

THE DAZZLING LIGHT

*The new head-covering is made of heavy steel, which has been specially treated to increase its resisting power. The walls protecting the skull are particularly thick, and the weight of the helmet renders its use in open warfare out of the question. The rim is large, like that of the headpiece of Mambrino, and the soldier can at will either bring the helmet forward and protect his eyes or wear it so as to protect the base of the skull. . . . Military experts admit that a continuance of the present trench warfare may lead to those engaged in it, especially bombing parties and barbed wire cutters, being more heavily armoured than the knights who fought at Bouvines and at Agincourt.—*THE TIMES, *July* 22, 1915.

THE war is already a fruitful mother of legends. Some people think that there are too many war legends, and a Croydon gentleman—or lady, I am not sure which—wrote to me quite recently telling me that a certain particular legend, which I will not specify, had become the "chief horror of the war." There may be something to be said for this point of view, but it strikes me as interesting that the old myth-making faculty has survived into these days, a relic of noble, far-off Homeric battles. And after all, what do we know? It does not do to be too sure that this, that, or the other hasn't happened and couldn't have happened.

What follows, at any rate, has no claim to be considered either as legend or as myth. It is merely one of the odd circumstances of these times, and I have no doubt it can easily be "explained away." In fact, the rationalistic explanation of the whole thing is patent and on the surface. There is only one little difficulty, and that, I fancy, is by no means insuperable. In any case this one knot or tangle may be put down as a queer coincidence and nothing more.

Here, then, is the curiosity or oddity in question. . A young fellow, whom we will call for avoidance of all identification Delamere Smith—he is now Lieutenant Delamere Smith—was spending his holidays on the coast of west South Wales at the beginning of the war. He was something or other not very important in the City, and in his leisure hours he smattered lightly and agreeably a little literature, a little art, a little antiquarianism. He liked the Italian primitives, he knew the difference between first, second, and third pointed, he had looked through Boutell's "Engraved Brasses." He had been heard indeed to speak with enthusiasm of the brasses of Sir Robert de Septvans and Sir Roger de Trumpington.

One morning—he thinks it must have been the morning of August 16, 1914— the sun shone so brightly into his room that he woke early, and the fancy took him that it would be fine to sit on the cliffs in the pure sunlight. So he dressed and went out, and climbed up Giltar Point, and sat there enjoying the sweet air and the radiance of the sea, and the sight of the fringe of creaming foam about the grey foundations of St. Margaret's Island. Then he looked beyond and gazed at the new white monastery on Caldy, and wondered who the architect was, and how he had contrived to make the group of buildings look exactly like the background of a mediæval picture.

After about an hour of this and a couple of pipes, Smith confesses that he began

to feel extremely drowsy. He was just
wondering whether it would not be pleasant to stretch himself out on the wild
thyme that scented the high place and go
to sleep till breakfast, when the mounting
sun caught one of the monastery windows,
and Smith stared sleepily at the darting
flashing light till it dazzled him. Then
he felt "queer." There was an odd sen-
sation as if the top of his head were dilat-
ing and contracting, and then he says he
had a sort of shock, something between
a mild current of electricity and the sensa-
tion of putting one's hand into the ripple
of a swift brook.

Now, what happened next Smith cannot describe at all clearly. He knew he
was on Giltar, looking across the waves to
Caldy; he heard all the while the hollow,
booming tide in the caverns of the rocks
far below him. And yet he saw, as if in
a glass, a very different country—a level

fenland cut by slow streams, by long
avenues of trimmed trees.

"It looked," he says, "as if it ought to
have been a lonely country, but it was
swarming with men; they were thick as
ants in an anthill. And they were all
dressed in armour; that was the strange
thing about it.

"I thought I was standing by what
looked as if it had been a farmhouse;
but it was all battered to bits, just a heap
of ruins and rubbish. All that was left
was one tall round chimney, shaped very
much like the fifteenth-century chimneys
in Pembrokeshire. And thousands and
tens of thousands went marching by.

"They were all in armour, and in all
sorts of armour. Some of them had over-
lapping tongues of bright metal fastened
on their clothes, others were in chain mail
from head to foot, others were in heavy
plate armour.

"They wore helmets of all shapes and sorts and sizes. One regiment had steel caps with wide brims, something like the old barbers' basins. Another lot had knights' tilting helmets on, closed up so that you couldn't see their faces. Most of them wore metal gauntlets, either of steel rings or plates, and they had steel over their boots. A great many had things like battle-maces swinging by their sides, and all these fellows carried a sort of string of big metal balls round their waist. Then a dozen regiments went by, every man with a steel shield slung over his shoulder. The last to go by were cross-bowmen."

In fact, it appeared to Delamere Smith that he watched the passing of a host of men in mediæval armour before him, and yet he knew—by the position of the sun and of a rosy cloud that was passing over the Worm's Head—that this vision, or whatever it was, lasted only a second or two. Then that slight sense of shock returned, and Smith returned to the contemplation of the physical phenomena of the Pembrokeshire coast—blue waves, grey St. Margaret's, and Caldy Abbey white in the sunlight.

It will be said, no doubt, and very likely with truth, that Smith fell asleep on Giltar, and mingled in a dream the thought of the great war just begun with his smatterings of mediæval battle and arms and armour. The explanation seems tolerable enough.

But there is the one little difficulty. It has been said that Smith is now Lieutenant Smith. He got his commission last autumn, and went out in May. He happens to speak French rather well, and so he has become what is called, I believe, an officer of liaison, or some such term. Anyhow, he is often behind the French lines.

He was home on short leave last week, and said:

"Ten days ago I was ordered to ——. I got there early in the morning, and had to wait a bit before I could see the General. I looked about me, and there on the left of us was a farm shelled into a heap of ruins, with one round chimney standing, shaped like the 'Flemish' chimneys in Pembrokeshire. And then the men in armour marched by, just as I had seen them—French regiments. The things like battle-maces were bomb-throwers, and the metal balls round the men's waists were the bombs. They told me that the cross-bows were used for bomb-shooting.

"The march I saw was part of a big movement; you will hear more of it before long."

THE BOWMEN AND
OTHER NOBLE GHOSTS

BY "THE LONDONER"

THERE was a journalist—and the
Evening News reader well knows
the initials of his name— who lately sat
down to write a story.

.   .   .   .   .

OF course his story had to be about the
war; there are no other stories nowadays.
And so he wrote of English soldiers who,
in the dusk on a field of France, faced the
sullen mass of the on-coming Huns.
They were few against fearful odds, but,
as they sent the breech-bolt home and
aimed and fired, they became aware that

others fought beside them. Down the
air came cries to St. George and twanging
of the bow-string; the old bowmen of
England had risen at England's need
from their graves in that French earth
and were fighting for England.

·   ·   ·   ·   ·

HE said that he made up that story by
himself, that he sat down and wrote it
out of his head.   But others knew better.
It must really have happened. There
was, I remember, a clergyman of good
credit who told him that he was clean
mistaken; the archers had really and truly
risen up to fight for England: the tale was
all up and down the front.

·   ·   ·   ·   ·

FOR my part I had thought that he wrote
out of his head; I had seen him at the
detestable job of doing it. I myself have
hated this business of writing ever since

I found out that it was not so easy as it looks, and I can always spare a little sympathy for a man who is driving a pen to the task of putting words in their right places. Yet the clergyman persuaded me at last. Who am I that I should doubt the faith of a clerk in holy orders? It must have happened. Those archers fought for us, and the grey-goose feather has flown once again in English battle.

.   .   .   .   .

SINCE that day I look eagerly for the ghosts who must be taking their share in this world-war. Never since the world began was such a war as this: surely Marlborough and the Duke, Talbot and Harry of Monmouth, and many another shadowy captain must be riding among our horsemen. The old gods of war are wakened by this loud clamour of the guns.

.   .   .   .   .

ALL the lands are astir.   It is not enough that Asia should be humming like an angry hive and the far islands in arms, Australia sending her young men and Canada making herself a camp. When we talk over the war news we call up ancient names: we debate how Rome stands and what is the matter with Greece.

.   .   .   .   .

As for Greece, I have ceased to talk of her.   If I wanted to say anything about Greece I should get down the Poetry Book and quote Lord Byron's fine old ranting verse. "The mountains look on Marathon—and Marathon looks on the sea." But "standing on the Persians' grave" Greece seems in the same humour that made Lord Byron give her up as a hopelessly flabby country.

.   .   .   .   .

"'Tis Greece, but living Greece no more" is as true as ever it was. That last telegram of the Kaiser must have done its soothing work. You remember how it ran: the Kaiser was too busy to make up new phrases. He telegraphed to his sister the familiar Potsdam sentence: "Woe to those who dare to draw the sword against me." I am sure that I have heard that before. And he added— delightful and significant postscript!— "My compliments to Tino."

.   .   .   .   .

And Tino—King Constantine of the Hellenes—understood. He is in bed now with a very bad cold, and like to stay in bed until the weather be more settled. But before going to bed he was able to tell a journalist that Greece was going quietly on with her proper business; it was her mission to carry civilization to the world.

Truly that was the mission of ancient Greece. What we get from Tino's modern Greece is not civilization but the little black currants for plum-cake.

. . . . .

BUT Rome. Greece may be dead or in the currant trade. Rome is alive and immortal. Do not talk to me about Signor Giolitti, who is quite sure that the only things that matter in this new Italy, which is old Rome, are her commercial relations with Germany. Rome of the legions, our ancient mistress and conqueror, is alive today, and she cannot be for an ignoble peace. Here in my newspaper is the speech of a poet spoken in Rome to a shouting crowd: I will cut out the column and put it in the Poetry Book.

. . . . .

HE calls to the living and to the dead: "I saw the fire of Vesta, O Romans, lit yesterday in the great steel works of Liguria. The fountain of Juturna, O Romans, I saw its water run to temper armour, to chill the drills that hollow out the bore of guns." This is poetry of the old Roman sort. I imagine that scene in Rome: the latest poet of Rome calling upon the Romans in the name of Vesta's holy fire, in the name of the springs at which the Great Twin Brethren washed their horses. I still believe in the power and the ancient charm of noble words. I do not think that Giolitti and the stock-brokers will keep old Rome off the old roads where the legions went.

POSTSCRIPT

WHILE this volume was passing through the press, Mr. Ralph Shirley, the editor of THE OCCULT REVIEW *called my attention to an article that is appearing in the August issue of his magazine, and was kind enough to let me see the advance proof sheets.*

The article is called "The Angelic Leaders." It is written by Miss Phyllis Campbell. I have read it with great care.

Miss Campbell says that she was in France when the war broke out. She became a nurse, and while she was nursing the wounded she was informed that an English soldier wanted a "holy picture." She went to the man and found him to be a Lancashire Fusilier. He said that he was a Wesleyan Methodist, and asked "for a picture or medal (he didn't care which) of St. George . . . because he had seen him on a white horse, leading the British at Vitry-le-François, when the Allies turned."

This statement was corroborated by a wounded R.F.A. man who was present. He saw a tall man with yellow hair, in golden armour, on a white horse, holding his sword up, and his mouth open as if he was saying, "Come on, boys! I'll put the kybosh on the devils." This figure was bareheaded—as appeared later from the testimony of other soldiers—and the R.F.A. man and the Fusilier knew that he was St. George, because he was exactly like the figure of St. George on the sovereigns. "Hadn't they seen him with his sword on every 'quid' they'd ever had?"

From further evidence it seemed that while the English had seen the apparition of St. George coming out of a "yellow mist" or "cloud of light," to the French had been vouchsafed visions of St. Michael the Archangel and Joan of Arc. Miss Campbell says:

> *"Everybody has seen them who has fought through from Mons to Ypres; they all agree on them individually, and have no doubt at all as to the final issue of their interference."*

Such are the main points of the article as it concerns the great legend of "The Angels of Mons." I cannot say that the author has shaken my incredulity—firstly, because the evidence is second-hand. Miss Campbell is perhaps acquainted with "Pickwick," and I would remind her of that famous (and golden) ruling of Stareleigh, J.: to the effect that you mustn't tell us what the soldier said; it's not evidence. Miss Campbell has offended against this rule, and she has not only told us what the soldier said, but she has omitted to give us the soldier's name and address.

If Miss Campbell proffered herself as a witness at the Old Bailey and said, "John Doe is undoubtedly guilty. A soldier I met told me that he had seen the prisoner put his hand into an old gentleman's pocket and take out a purse"—well, she would find that the stout spirit of Mr. Justice Stareleigh still survives in our judges.

The soldier must be produced. Before that is done we are not technically aware that he exists at all.

Then there are one or two points in the article itself which puzzle me. The Fusilier and the R.F.A. man had seen St. George "leading the British at Vitry-le-François, when the Allies turned." Thus the time of the apparition and the place of the apparition were firmly fixed in the two soldiers' minds.

Yet the very next paragraph in the article begins:

"'Where was this?' I asked. But neither of them could tell."

This is an odd circumstance. They knew, and yet they did not know; or, rather, they had forgotten a piece of information that they had themselves imparted a few seconds before.

Another point. The soldiers knew that the figure on the horse was St. George by his exact likeness to the figure of the saint on the English sovereign.

This, again, is odd. The apparition was of a bareheaded figure in golden armour. The St. George of the coinage is naked, except for a short cape flying from the shoulders, and a helmet. He is not bareheaded, and has no armour—save the piece on his head. I do not quite see how the soldiers were so certain as to the identity of the apparition.

Lastly, Miss Campbell declares that "everybody" who fought from Mons to Ypres saw the apparitions. If that be so, it is again odd that Nobody has come forward to testify at first hand to the most amazing event of his life. Many men have been back on leave from the front, we have many wounded in hospital, many soldiers have written letters home. And they have all combined, this great host, to keep silence as to the most wonderful of occurrences, the most inspiring assurance, the surest omen of victory.

It may be so, but——

ARTHUR MACHEN.